★ **GREAT SPORTS TEAMS** ★

THE PHILADELPHIA
FLYERS
HOCKEY TEAM

Glen Macnow

RENFROE MIDDLE SCHOOL
220 WEST COLLEGE AVE.
DECATUR, GEORGIA 30030

Enslow Publishers, Inc.
40 Industrial Road   PO Box 38
Box 398   Aldershot
Berkeley Heights, NJ 07922   Hants GU12 6BP
USA   UK
http://www.enslow.com

Copyright © 2000 by Enslow Publishers, Inc.

All rights reserved.

No part of this book may be reproduced by any means without the written permission of the publisher.

Library of Congress Cataloging-in-Publication Data

Macnow, Glen.
 The Philadelphia Flyers hockey team / Glen Macnow.
   p. cm. — (Great sports teams)
 Includes bibliographical references and index.
 Summary: Traces the history of the National Hockey League team that earned the nickname "The Broad Street Bullies" in the 1970s for its rough play.
   ISBN 0-7660-1279-4
   1. Philadelphia Flyers (Hockey team)—History—Juvenile literature.
 [1. Philadelphia Flyers (Hockey team)—History. 2. Hockey—History.]
 I. Title. II. Series.
 GV848.P48M33   2000
 796.962'64'0974811—dc21   99-12581
                                                                CIP

Printed in the United States of America

10 9 8 7 6 5 4 3 2 1

To Our Readers: All Internet addresses in this book were active and appropriate when we went to press. Any comments or suggestions can be sent by e-mail to Comments@enslow.com or to the address on the back cover.

Illustration Credits: AP/Wide World Photos

Cover Illustration: AP/Wide World Photos

CONTENTS

1. Power and Speed 5
2. Broad Street Bullies 11
3. Flyers Aces 17
4. Flyers Leaders 23
5. High Flying Teams 29
6. Ready to Launch 35

Statistics 40

Chapter Notes 43

Glossary 45

Further Reading 46

Index 47

Where to Write 48

Eric Lindros had to face his boyhood idol, Mark Messier, and the New York Rangers in the 1997 Eastern Conference Finals. Lindros more than held his own against this legendary player.

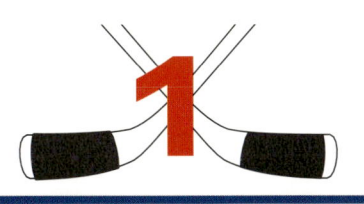

POWER AND SPEED

The puck slid toward Eric Lindros's stick with ten seconds left in a tie game. Just as Lindros took the pass in front of the New York Rangers net, an opposing defenseman pushed his glove into Lindros's face.

Time Running Out

Now there were nine seconds left in regulation. Lindros shook off the defenseman and moved to his backhand. Eight seconds.

Lindros faked a shot that sent Rangers goalie Mike Richter to his left. Seven seconds. As Richter moved, Lindros rifled a backhand toward the empty side of the net and . . .

. . . SCORE!

With just 6.8 seconds left, Lindros's bullet gave his Philadelphia Flyers a 3–2 win over the Rangers. What a clutch goal it was. Coming in Game 4 of the National Hockey League's 1997 Eastern Conference Finals made it even bigger. The goal gave the Flyers the lead, three games to one, over the archrival Rangers.

On to the Finals

The Flyers went on to win Game 5 and the series. In the clincher, Flyers center Rod Brind'Amour scored two big goals. Lindros bulled his way past Rangers captain Mark Messier to score an insurance goal late in the game. The win put the Flyers in the 1997 Stanley Cup Finals.

"We just lost to a great team," Messier said afterward. "Those Flyers are big and fast and very deep. They're a young team, too. They'll be dangerous for a lot of years to come."[1]

The Flyers fell short in the Stanley Cup Finals that year. They were swept by the Detroit Red Wings. But Philadelphia made its mark as a team that will be heard from for years to come.

Big, Fast, and Strong

Led by Lindros and teammate John LeClair, the Flyers of the late 1990s were a team that could beat opponents with power and speed. One moment, Lindros was grinding his way between two big defensemen. The next, LeClair was firing a bullet over a hapless goalie's shoulder. And with both men being the size of NFL linebackers, few opponents were strong enough to contain them.

Those two superstars were complemented by players such as Brind'Amour, a smart, rugged player who played every single game for five straight seasons.

Flyers assistant captain, Rod Brind'Amour came up big against the Rangers. He is shown here beating Rangers goalie Mike Richter in Game 3.

Goalie Ron Hextall was a vocal leader who loved the pressure of big games. In front of Hextall stood solid defensemen such as Chris Therien and Eric Desjardins.

"I think our club has the talent to contend every season," Lindros said in 1997. "Of course, we won't be satisfied until we win it all."[2]

On the Doorstep

Recently, they came close to winning the Cup several times. In 1997, they went to the finals once again. In 1996, they finished with the best regular-season record in the Eastern Conference but lost to the Florida Panthers in the playoff semifinals.

The Flyers have a proud tradition. They entered the NHL in 1967 and won their division in their very first year. For seventeen straight seasons—from 1972–73 to 1988–89—they made the NHL playoffs. Two times—in 1974 and 1975—they won the Stanley Cup.

Continuing a Rich Tradition

Three Hall of Fame players have worn the Flyers' orange-and-black jersey. Goalie Bernie Parent was the best goalie of the 1970s, with a cat-quick glove hand. Center Bobby Clarke had a lot of talent and even more grit. Some regard Clarke as the greatest team leader ever to play hockey. And left-winger Bill Barber retired after fourteen seasons with the most career goals (420) scored by a Flyers player.

The Flyers have come close to bringing the Stanley Cup back to Philadelphia. But close is not good enough for this team. Consider, for example, the ending of one of the most exciting contests in franchise history—Game 5 of the 1997 Eastern Conference Finals against the Rangers.

The Flyers went into the night leading the series, three games to one. After two periods on the ice at Philadelphia's CoreStates Center, each team had scored two goals. Midway through the third period, Brind'Amour checked Rangers superstar Wayne Gretzky off the puck. Brind'Amour spun around, eluded New York defenseman Bruce Driver, and skated in alone on Richter. Brind'Amour moved the puck back and forth on his stick, waited for Richter to flop to the ice, and shot it over the goalie's shoulder for the

After the thrilling conclusion to Game 5, the Flyers celebrated the series win. Number twenty-seven is goalie Ron Hextall, and twenty-eight is defenseman Kjell Samuelsson.

winning goal. A few minutes later, Brind'Amour slapped one in from the face-off circle to seal the win—and the series.

At game's end, Lindros skated to center ice. He was handed the Prince of Wales Trophy as captain of the best team in the NHL's Eastern Conference. But he refused to take the trophy. "I wasn't touching it," he said afterward. "I wasn't going near it. We haven't won anything yet."[3]

The only trophy he wants to hold when he skates around the ice in Philadelphia is the Stanley Cup. Until then, he said, nothing else counts.

Power and Speed

Dave "The Hammer" Schultz (#8) was one of the toughest players in the NHL. Because of players such as Schultz, the Flyers of the 1970s and 1980s were known as the Broad Street Bullies.

2

BROAD STREET BULLIES

The history of pro hockey in Philadelphia begins with a team known as the Quakers. They joined the National Hockey League in 1930. The Quakers won just four of their 44 games that season. Perhaps that is why they folded after just one season.

After that, seven minor-league hockey teams tried and failed in Philly. The local fans were used to big-time clubs in baseball, football, and basketball. A second-rate team would not do.

Getting Off the Ground

The city's second chance with the NHL came in 1965. The league decided to double in size from six teams to twelve. A local businessman named Ed Snider heard about the expansion plans. Snider had just attended his first hockey game in New York City—and loved it.

He paid the $1 million entry fee and was welcomed into the NHL.

First, the team needed a name. A contest was held, and fans suggested two hundred ideas. The possibilities included the Ramblers, Liberty Bells, Blizzards, and Bruisers. Flyers—suggested by a nine-year-old boy—was chosen because it suggested speed and action.

Early Success

The Flyers played their first game in 1967. Their roster came from players drafted from existing NHL clubs. The first player they took was twenty-two-year-old goalie Bernie Parent of the Boston Bruins. It was a great pick. Parent went on to star in two Stanley Cup triumphs and was voted into the Hockey Hall of Fame.

In their first season, the Flyers played in the NHL's Western Division, along with five other new clubs. Led by speedy forwards Leon Rochefort and Lou Angotti, the Flyers finished first in the division of newcomers. The good beginning, however, was not without disaster. Late in the season, the roof of the Flyers' home arena, the Spectrum, was blown off during a snowstorm. The team had to play its remaining home games seven hundred miles away in Quebec City, in Quebec, Canada—not a great treat for their hometown fans.

The Right Choice

The team slumped over the next few seasons. But something was being built for the future. In 1969, the franchise drafted nineteen-year-old center Bobby Clarke from Flin Flon, Manitoba, Canada, with the seventeenth pick of the amateur draft. Clarke was regarded as a great talent, but other teams passed on him because he had diabetes, which they thought might weaken him.[1] The Flyers were not worried about this. Clarke turned out to be one of the greatest hockey players of all time.

In 1972, the Flyers suffered one of the lowest moments in team history, in a game against the St. Louis Blues. It wasn't just that they lost the game, 4–1.

In the 1980s the Flyers reached the Stanley Cup Finals three times. One of the star players was defenseman Mark Howe (left), shown here with his father, Hall of Famer Gordie Howe.

Broad Street Bullies

*E*ric Lindros has led the Flyers resurgence in the 1990s. Big and strong, Lindros beats his opponents with both talent and strength.

The Blues—known as a rough and nasty team at the time—beat up the Flyers so badly that they almost ran from the rink. Owner Ed Snider was embarrassed to see his team in fear of another. "I made up my mind that we needed to get big, tough players," he said.[2]

Toughening Up

Within two years, the Flyers were the biggest, baddest group of players in the NHL. With battlers such as Dave "The Hammer" Schultz, Bob Kelly, and Moose Dupont, they became known as the Broad Street Bullies. With those players providing the muscle—and Clarke and Parent providing the skill—the Flyers won the Stanley Cup in 1974 and 1975.

Over the years, the Flyers have stayed big and tough. They are no longer the Bullies, but they have used power more than speed to amass the NHL's second-best overall record since 1970. Only the Montreal Canadiens have done better. The Flyers' greatest players have been large, strong men, such as Tim Kerr and Brian Propp in the 1980s, followed by Eric Lindros and John LeClair in the 1990s. There has been another constant: top-rate goaltending. After Bernie Parent retired in 1979, he was followed by All-Star goalies Pete Peeters, Pelle Lindbergh, and Ron Hextall.

The Flyers have not won the title since 1975. But there have been great highlights: Five times, they got back to the Stanley Cup Finals, only to lose. In 1979, the Flyers ran off a thirty-five-game unbeaten streak—the longest in professional sports.[3]

Bernie Parent is considered to be one of the best goaltenders of all time. The Flyers retired Parent's uniform number one.

FLYERS ACES

Hundreds of players have proudly worn the orange-and-black Flyers uniform over the years. The roster has included great scorers like Bobby Clarke, Tim Kerr, and Eric Lindros. There have been solid defensemen, such as Ed Van Impe, Mark Howe, and Eric Desjardins.

Philadelphia's consistently strongest position has been in the nets. From the franchise's birth in 1967 through the 1990s, the Flyers have been blessed with strong goaltending.

Bernie Parent

The best—and one of the tops in hockey history—was Bernie Parent. During the 1970s, Parent played between the pipes with such style and grace that he appeared to be performing a ballet. For two years in a row, he swept three major awards—the Vezina Trophy (for top goalie), the Conn Smythe Trophy (for Most

Valuable Player in the playoffs), and the award for the NHL's first-team All-Star goaltender. In 1973–74, he won 47 games, an all-time NHL record.

Parent, known as Bennie to his teammates, started as a kid in Montreal, kicking rubber balls out of goals while wearing galoshes.[1] He came into the NHL with the Boston Bruins but he was not very impressive. The Flyers picked him in the 1967 expansion draft that stocked the team.

He instantly became the city's most popular player. When the Flyers were a bad team, Parent's great play kept them in games. When the team improved, he led them to a higher level. In the two seasons that the Flyers won the Stanley Cup, Parent recorded astounding goals-against averages of 1.89 and 2.02, as well as 12 shutouts each season.

"He was the best ever," said Bobby Taylor, his longtime backup. "The only goalie ever who could come close was Glenn Hall."[2]

Tragically, Parent's career was ended by injury. In 1979, an opponent's stick accidentally sliced his eyelid. He retired within weeks. Five years later, he became the first Flyers player elected to the Hockey Hall of Fame.

Pelle Lindbergh

Tragedy would also strike the Flyers' next great goalie. Pelle Lindbergh grew up in Sweden. At age twelve, he watched films of the Flyers and decided that Parent was his hero. By 1981, he was standing in Parent's old

Flyers goaltender Pelle Lindbergh deflects the puck away from his net. Defenseman Mark Howe wards off Chicago center Troy Murray.

goalie crease in the Spectrum in Philadelphia. Four years later, he too would win the Vezina Trophy.

Lindbergh had incredible reflexes. Shooters would aim at the space between his bowed legs, but they would be disappointed when the pads closed as quickly as a blinking eye. His balance was excellent. His glove hand was as soft as his easygoing personality.

In 1985, Lindbergh died in a late-night car crash near Philadelphia. He had been drinking alcohol and, by several accounts, revved his Porsche up to 110 miles per hour before hitting a brick wall. It was the saddest moment in Flyers history.

Using his quick reflexes, Ron Hextall knocks the puck away from the net. Hextall is known for having excellent stick-handling ability.

"You don't replace a Pelle Lindbergh," General Manager Bobby Clarke said the following season.[3] Certainly, Lindbergh as a man could not be replaced. But the Flyers had discovered a quick and colorful rookie who could fill the job on the ice. His name was Ron Hextall.

Ron Hextall

Hextall was a six-foot three-inch youngster who played goalie unlike anyone before him in NHL history. He chopped at opponents' legs like Paul Bunyan clearing a forest. He threw outlet passes like Hakeem Olajuwon. He coaxed other teams into brawls.

More than anything else, Hextall stopped the puck. He won the Vezina Trophy as a rookie in 1987. That same year, he won the Conn Smythe Trophy as the playoffs' Most Valuable Player—even though the Flyers lost to the Edmonton Oilers in Game 7 of the Stanley Cup Finals. It marked just the second time in NHL history that a member of the losing team had won that award.

"I guess we beat him in the end," said Edmonton's Wayne Gretzky. "But I'll have nightmares about Hextall for years to come."[4]

Hextall played his first six seasons with the Flyers. He was traded, but returned two years later. For four more seasons in Philadelphia, he was still causing opponents to come away from the game with nightmares.

Flyers Aces

Flyers head coach Fred Shero carries the Stanley Cup down a plane ramp. Fans were awaiting the team's arrival to begin celebrating Philadelphia's 1975 Stanley Cup championship.

4

FLYERS LEADERS

The Flyers had a dozen coaches in their first thirty-two seasons. Of these coaches, three excellent men stand out.

Fred Shero

The first is Fred Shero, the top coach in team history. Shero led the Flyers to two Stanley Cup championships. Even his players would tell you that his coaching—more than their own skill—earned the team its titles.

"Freddie did more with less than anyone in NHL history," said Dave Schultz, a winger on those teams. "Look at the lineup we had when the Flyers won in 1974. There were only four players on the whole team who could legitimately be called special talents."[1] The rest of them were seemingly average.

Once a promising player, Shero had to retire because of an injured back. He turned to coaching. He spent fourteen years in the minors before getting his NHL break with the Flyers in 1971.

Few had ever seen anyone like him. Shero studied hockey strategies as if they were plans for military formations. He was the first NHL coach to travel to the Soviet Union to learn the innovative methods of that nation's coaches. He would run his players through unique drills—twelve-on-twelve games, for example—to keep them from getting bored with practice.

"Hockey is a children's game played by men," Shero said. "Since it is a children's game, they ought to have fun."[2]

Shero's nickname was Freddie the Fog, because he always seemed to be in a daze. One night, in Atlanta, Shero took a walk down a corridor between periods to plot strategy. Deep in thought, he took a left turn, opened a door, and kept walking. Finally, Shero figured out his plan for the next period. Unfortunately, he had walked right out of the rink and into the parking lot. He found himself locked out of the game when the next period began.[3]

A strange man, perhaps, but very successful, Shero led the Flyers to titles in 1974 and 1975. The next season, they lost in the Stanley Cup Finals to the Montreal Canadiens. But they played their best season ever, compiling 51 wins, 13 losses, and 16 ties, for a total of 118 points.

Pat Quinn

Soon after Shero left in 1978, the club promoted minor-league coach Pat Quinn. He taught a new system that relied on forechecking pressure from all three forwards. The idea was to try to create turnovers in

*P*at Quinn was head coach of the Flyers from 1978 to 1982. He led the Flyers to the 1980 Stanley Cup Finals and was the skipper during the teams 35-game unbeaten streak.

the other team's defensive zone. It was a risky strategy that put extra demands on the two defensemen and the goalie. But the team quickly caught on.

In the 1979–80 season, the Flyers had an amazing accomplishment. After a 1–1 start, they began a streak that is still unmatched in pro sports. Over the next eighty-four days, they refused to lose. They won 25 games and tied 10. Their record at the start of January 1980 was 36–1–10.

Even opposing coaches were amazed by Quinn's team. "You look at the travel, the schedule, and the balance of the league, and that streak is impossible," said Scotty Bowman, who was coaching the Buffalo Sabres. "But it's not impossible. They've done it."[4]

Pro sports' longest unbeaten streak ended at 35 games. Quinn led the Flyers back to the Stanley Cup Finals that season. Philadelphia lost the series to the New York Islanders in six games.

Mike Keenan

The third memorable coach in Flyers team history was Mike Keenan. On his 1984 job application, Keenan wrote, "The more I win, the more I want to win. Nothing short of this is acceptable."[5]

That was how he coached—as if losing were the worst crime in the world. "Iron" Mike Keenan was controlling and sometimes a bully. He didn't show any sense of humor. But he could scare his players into playing well. And he had great intuition—for example, when he gave the starting goalie job to twenty-two-year-old rookie Ron Hextall in 1986.

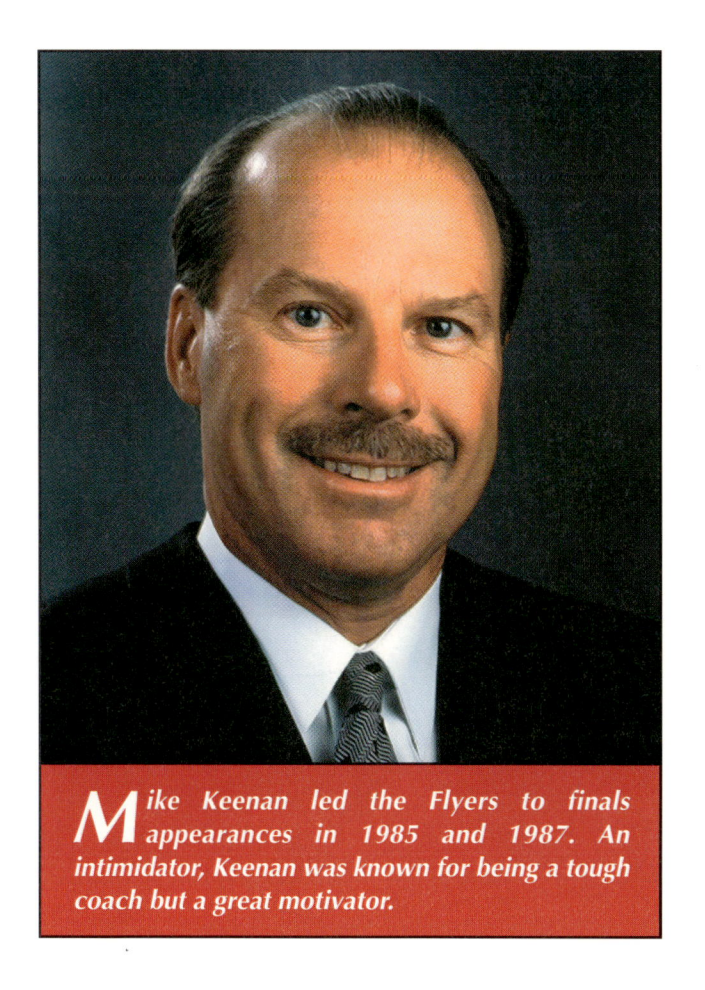

*M*ike Keenan led the Flyers to finals appearances in 1985 and 1987. An intimidator, Keenan was known for being a tough coach but a great motivator.

Keenan's teams were hurt by injuries and old age. They peaked at the same time as Wayne Gretzky's Edmonton Oilers, perhaps the best club in NHL history. Twice finalists, the Flyers were good enough to win in other eras, but they couldn't master Gretzky and the Oilers. Still, the Flyers were driven, organized, and tough.

"We reinforced the Philadelphia image," said defenseman Brad Marsh. "We weren't the Broad Street Bullies, but we had a bunch of hardworking talented guys. It's unfortunate we didn't win. We came so close."[6]

Flyers Leaders

Flyers teams of the 1970s were known for their toughness. Here, Philadelphia squares off against members of the Boston Bruins during the 1974 Stanley Cup finals.

5

HIGH FLYING TEAMS

Great teams have won the NHL championship in many ways. There have been fantastic skating teams, such as the Edmonton Oilers of the 1980s. There have been solid defensive teams, such as the 1995 New Jersey Devils. There have been shooting teams and passing teams. The Flyers of the mid-1970s won two titles. They won them on sheer toughness.

Only the Strong Survive

Philadelphia is called the City of Brotherly Love. But under Coach Fred Shero, the Flyers earned Philly another nickname—the City of Brotherly Shove. The team was called the Broad Street Bullies, because of the address of their home arena, the Spectrum, and their bruising style of play.

Shero built a team of big, nasty men who viewed hockey as not much different from professional boxing. They had colorful nicknames—Dave "The Hammer"

Schultz, Bob "Hound" Kelly, Andre "Moose" Dupont, and Don "Big Bird" Saleski. It was a team of role players who knew they did not have as much skill as some other NHL clubs, but who came to battle every game. Many of those games ended in brawls, with the Bullies winning both the fights and on the scoreboard.

"The fighting brought us together as a team," said Schultz. "Soon it was clear that other teams were backing off from us almost as if it were a conditioned reflex. We forced them to give us respect."[1]

1973-74

During the 1973–74 NHL season, the Flyers set an NHL record for penalty minutes. But they also emerged as winners, racking up 112 points in the 78-game regular season. First, they breezed past the Atlanta Flames and the New York Rangers to get to the Stanley Cup finals. Then, they took out the dangerous Boston Bruins in six games to take the coveted Stanley Cup. The sixth game ended in a 1–0 victory, as Bruins superstar Bobby Orr slammed his stick on the ice in frustration.

The 1973–74 title marked the first time an NHL expansion team had won the Stanley Cup. Two million people crowded along Broad Street in Philadelphia for the victory parade. The *Philadelphia Inquirer* ran this front-page headline: "Miracle Flyers Take the Cup and City Goes Wild with Joy."[2]

1974-75

The city went wild again the following year, when the Flyers beat the dangerous Buffalo Sabres, four games to two, to repeat as NHL champions.

Flyers left wing Bob Kelly blasts a shot past Buffalo goalie Gerry Desjardins. Kelly was instrumental in helping Philly beat the Sabres to win the Stanley Cup in 1975.

The final game was a classic goaltenders' battle between Philly's Bernie Parent and Buffalo's Roger Crozier. Each made more than thirty saves, some of them unbelievable. The game was scoreless into the third period, when Flyers captain Bobby Clarke shot a puck that wound up sitting on the back of Buffalo's net. While the Sabres waited for a referee's whistle, Flyers winger Bob Kelly skated behind the net and poked the puck free. Kelly swung around the front of the net while the stunned Sabres stood and watched. He beat the goalie along the ice just inside the far post.

High Flying Teams

The Flyers added an insurance goal, but Parent did not need it, as they won, 2–0.

Winning one title was tremendous. Winning two seemed unbelievable.

Although the Bullies will be remembered for their toughness, there were some supremely talented players on the squad. Goalie Bernie Parent was one of the NHL's dominant goaltenders of the era. Forwards Rick MacLeish and Reggie Leach could score 50 goals a season. Winger Bill Barber was a hard skater with a beautiful wrist shot and a knack for drawing the other team into penalties. Parent and Barber would wind up in the Hockey Hall of Fame.

Bobby Clarke

Center and captain Bobby Clarke is also in the Hall of Fame. He was the glue that held the Flyers together in their championship years. In fact, he was awarded the Hart Trophy as the NHL's Most Valuable Player three times in his career.

Clarke came to the Flyers from Flin Flon, Manitoba, Canada, in 1969. Because he had diabetes, some scouts thought he would not be strong enough to play in the NHL. How wrong they were! During a fifteen-season career—all spent with the Flyers—Clarke scored 358 goals and assisted on 852 others. He still holds all of the team's major scoring records.

More important, Clarke played full throttle on every shift. He was the ultimate hustler, the ultimate clutch player, and the ultimate motivator of his teammates.

Flyers center Bobby Clarke was one of the greatest scorers and team leaders in NHL history. Clarke scored 1,210 points in his Hall of Fame career.

"I don't think there has ever been another player to have such an influence on a team," said Coach Shero. "Other superstars whose teams have won were inspirational, no doubt. But Bobby lifted an expansion team to a championship for the first time. He's the best leader I've ever seen."[3]

Clarke is back with the Flyers. Today, he is the club's president and general manager, trying to bring the Stanley Cup back to Philadelphia. His biggest challenge is finding men who play with the heart of a Bobby Clarke.

John LeClair, number ten, knocks Tampa Bay's John Cullen to the ice after a fight for the puck. After joining the Flyers in 1995, LeClair blossomed into one of the league's best goal scorers.

6
READY TO LAUNCH

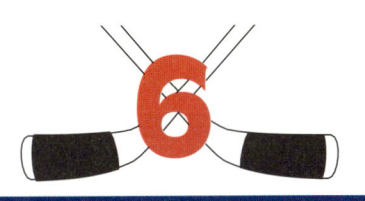

Philadelphia has not hosted a title parade for the Flyers since 1975, but the Flyers have come close. The team has made it back to the Stanley Cup Finals five times since then, most recently in 1997. Each time they lost. The word around Philadelphia, however, is that the drought could end soon.

A Strong Team

Through the 1990s, the Flyers put together the nucleus of an outstanding club. Bobby Clarke—their star player of earlier years—returned to the franchise as general manager. Clarke engineered some trades that vaulted the club to the top of the NHL standings.

His best move came in 1995. Clarke traded Mark Recchi—a natural goal scorer—to the Montreal Canadiens for defenseman Eric Desjardins and left-winger John LeClair. Desjardins immediately became the leader of Philadelphia's power play and the team's steadiest defenseman. "I've seen Eric play 30 games in a row without making a mistake," said Flyers coach Roger Neilson.[1] Desjardins was chosen to play in three straight NHL All-Star games.

John LeClair

LeClair proved to be even better. In Montreal, the big (6 feet 2 inches, 220 pounds) winger from Vermont had a reputation as a lazy player. But in Philadelphia, he blossomed into a hard worker and a star. LeClair is a bull on skates, pushing past smaller opponents and using every ounce of energy on every shift. And like all great goal scorers, he has an ability to score from all angles and all over the ice. Once, he even scored when the puck bounced off his nose into the net.

In Philadelphia, LeClair has become a regular first-team NHL All-Star. He scored fifty or more goals three seasons in a row. No American-born player before him had accomplished that feat in the NHL.

"There aren't a lot of players in this league who scare me out there on the ice," said Detroit Red Wings defenseman Larry Murphy. "But LeClair is one of them. You know he's either going to hurt you by banging into you or by scoring on you. He can make you look downright silly."[2]

During his first two seasons with the Flyers, LeClair played on a dynamic line called the Legion of Doom. His right-winger was Mikael Renberg, a quick-skating goal scorer from Sweden. Before the 1997–98 season,

Renberg was traded to the Tampa Bay Lightning in exchange for center Chris Gratton.

LeClair's centerman, of course, is Eric Lindros.

Eric Lindros

Lindros came to Philadelphia in 1992 in a giant deal with the Quebec Nordiques. The Flyers traded six players, two draft picks, and $15 million to get the teenager who was called the Next One. Even before he played in the NHL, Lindros was compared with all-time stars such as Gordie Howe, Mark Messier, and Mario Lemieux.

Skating behind the net, Eric Lindros looks to make a play. Defending is Chris Chelios of the Chicago Blackhawks.

Ready to Launch

Flyers defenseman Eric Desjardins shields the puck from Alex Hicks of the Florida Panthers.

Has he lived up to that billing? In one way, no, because Lindros did not lead the Flyers to a Stanley Cup during his first seven seasons. However, he has emerged as one of hockey's brightest stars. Lindros, wearing his familiar number eighty-eight jersey, was voted the NHL's Most Valuable Player in 1995. That season, he tied for the league lead in scoring and led the Flyers to the Atlantic Division title. He has been the team's captain since 1994.

Lindros, like LeClair, is a football player wearing a hockey jersey. A six-feet five-inch, 235 pound center, Lindros is one of the NHL's largest players. "He is also one of the strongest and one of the meanest," said Coach Neilson. "Eric is able to create space for himself because other players are afraid to get near him. Can you blame them? Plus, he's a great skater, a great face-off man and has, perhaps, the quickest shot in the league."[3]

Hope for the Future

With Lindros, LeClair, and Desjardins as a nucleus, Flyers fans have plenty of reasons to be optimistic. Add in other talented players—such as center Rod Brind'Amour and defenseman Chris Therien—and there is good reason to believe that it won't be long until the Stanley Cup is once again carried along on a parade through downtown Philadelphia.

Ready to Launch

STATISTICS

Team Record

SEASON	SEASON RECORD	PLAYOFF RECORD	COACH	DIVISION FINISH
1967–68	031–32–11	3–4	Keith Allen	1st
1968–69	20–35–21	0–4	Keith Allen	3rd
1969–70	17–35–24	—	Vic Stasiuk	5th
1970–71	28–33–17	0–4	Vic Stasiuk	3rd
1971–72	26–38–14	—	Fred Shero	5th
1972–73	37–30–11	5–6	Fred Shero	2nd
1973–74	50–16–12	12–5	Fred Shero	1st
1974–75	51–18–11	12–5	Fred Shero	1st
1975–76	51–13–16	8–8	Fred Shero	1st
1976–77	48–16–16	4–6	Fred Shero	1st
1977–78	45–20–15	7–5	Fred Shero	2nd
1978–79	40–25–15	3–5	Bob McCammon / Pat Quinn	2nd
1979–80	48–12–20	13–6	Pat Quinn	1st
1980–81	41–24–15	6–6	Pat Quinn	2nd
1981–82	38–31–11	1–3	Pat Quinn / Bob McCammon	3rd
1982–83	49–23–8	0–3	Bob McCammon	1st
1983–84	44–26–10	0–3	Bob McCammon	3rd
1984–85	53–20–7	12–7	Mike Keenan	1st
1985–86	53–23–4	2–3	Mike Keenan	1st
1986–87	46–26–8	15–11	Mike Keenan	1st
1987–88	38–33–9	3–4	Mike Keenan	2nd
1988–89	36–36–8	10–9	Paul Holmgren	4th
1989–90	30–39–11	—	Paul Holmgren	6th
1990–91	33–37–10	—	Paul Holmgren	5th
1991–92	32–37–11	—	Paul Holmgren / Bill Dineen	6th

The Philadelphia Flyers Hockey Team

Team Record (con't)

SEASON	SEASON RECORD	PLAYOFF RECORD	COACH	DIVISION FINISH
1992–93	36–37–11	—	Bill Dineen	5th
1993–94	35–39–10	—	Terry Simpson	6th
1994–95	28–16–4	10–5	Terry Murray	1st
1995–96	45–24–13	6–6	Terry Murray	1st
1996–97	45–24–13	12–7	Terry Murray	2nd
1997–98	42–29–11	1–4	Wayne Cashman Roger Nielson	2nd
1998–99	37–26–19	2–4	Roger Nielson	2nd
Totals	1,253–873–396	147–133		

Coaching Records

COACH	YEARS COACHED	FLYERS RECORD	CHAMPIONSHIPS
Keith Allen	1967–69	51–67–32	West Division, 1968
Vic Stasiuk	1969–71	45–68–41	None
Fred Shero	1971–78	308–151–95	Stanley Cup, 1974, 1975 Wales Conference, 1976 Patrick Division, 1977
Bob McCammon	1978–79 1982–84	119–68–31	Patrick Division, 1983
Pat Quinn	1978–82	141–73–48	Wales Conference, 1980
Mike Keenan	1984–88	190–102–28	Wales Conference, 1985, 1987 Patrick Division, 1986
Paul Holmgren	1988–92	107–126–31	None
Bill Dineen	1992–93	60–60–20	None
Terry Simpson	1993–94	35–39–10	None
Terry Murray	1994–97	118–64–30	Atlantic Division, 1995, 1996 Eastern Conference, 1997
Wayne Cashman	1997–98	32–20–9	None
Roger Neilson	1998–99	47–35–21	None

Statistics

Great Skaters

CAREER STATISTICS

PLAYER	SEA	YRS	GAMES	G	A	PTS
Bill Barber‡	1972–84	12	903	420	463	883
Bobby Clarke‡	1969–84	15	1,144	358	852	1,210
Mark Howe*	1982–92	16	929	197	545	742
Tim Kerr	1980–91	13	655	370	304	674
John LeClair	1995–99	9	583	269	269	538
Eric Lindros	1992–99	7	431	263	337	600
Rick MacLeish	1970–81, 1983	14	846	349	410	759
Brian Propp	1979–89	15	1,016	425	579	1,004
Rick Tocchet	1984–92	14	909	385	436	821
Ed Van Impe	1967–75	11	700	27	126	153

SEA=Seasons with Flyers
YRS=Years in the NHL
GAMES=Games played
G=Goals
A=Assists
PTS=Points scored

Great Goalies

CAREER STATISTICS

PLAYER	SEA	YRS	GAMES	MIN	GA	SH	GAA
Ron Hextall	1986–92, 1994–99	13	608	34,749	1,723	23	2.98
Pelle Lindbergh	1981–86	5	157	9,151	503	7	3.30
Bernie Parent* ‡	1967–70, 1973–79	13	608	35,136	1,493	55	2.55
Pete Peeters	1978–82, 1989–91	13	489	27,699	1,424	21	3.08
Wayne Stephenson	1974–79	10	328	18,343	937	14	3.06

SEA=Seasons with Flyers
YRS=Years in the NHL
GAMES=Games played
MIN=Minutes played
GA=Goals against
SH=Shutouts
GAA=Goals against average

*Does not include World Hockey Association (WHA) statistics.
‡Member of Hockey Hall of Fame.

The Philadelphia Flyers Hockey Team

CHAPTER NOTES

Chapter 1. Power and Speed

1. Ray Parrillo, "Gretzky, Messier Feeling the Pain of Many Playoffs Past," *Philadelphia Inquirer*, May 26, 1997, p. F5.

2. Timothy Dwyer, "Lindros: Ordinary Guy with Extraordinary Talent," *Philadelphia Inquirer*, May 26, 1997, p. F1.

3. Ibid.

Chapter 2. Broad Street Bullies

1. Stan Fischler, *Bobby Clarke and the Ferocious Flyers* (New York: Dodd, Mead & Company, 1974), p. 11.

2. Jay Greenberg, *Full Spectrum: The Complete History of the Philadelphia Flyers Hockey Club* (Chicago: Triumph Books, 1996), p. 40.

3. Ibid., p. 378.

Chapter 3. Flyers Aces

1. Jay Greenberg, *Full Spectrum: The Complete History of the Philadelphia Flyers Hockey Club* (Chicago: Triumph Books, 1996), p. 84.

2. Ibid.

3. Gene Hart, *Score! My Twenty-five Years with the Broad Street Bullies* (Chicago: Bonus Books, Inc., 1996), p. 234.

4. Ibid., p. 240.

Chapter 4. Flyers Leaders

1. Dave Schultz, *The Hammer: Confessions of a Hockey Enforcer* (New York: Summit Books, 1981), p. 89.

2. Gene Hart, *Score! My Twenty-five Years with the Broad Street Bullies* (Chicago: Bonus Books, Inc., 1996), p. 101.

3. Stan Fischler, *Bobby Clarke and the Ferocious Flyers* (New York: Dodd, Mead & Company, 1974), p. 119.

4. Jay Greenberg, *Full Spectrum: The Complete History of the Philadelphia Flyers Hockey Club* (Chicago: Triumph Books, 1996), p. 212.

5. Ibid., p. 237.

6. Hart, p. 105.

Chapter 5. High Flying Teams

1. Dave Schultz, *The Hammer: Confessions of a Hockey Enforcer* (New York: Summit Books, 1981), p. 73.

2. Jack Chevalier, "Miracle Flyers Take the Cup and City Goes Wild with Joy," *Philadelphia Inquirer*, May 20, 1974, p. A1.

3. Frank Orr, Jay Greenberg, and Gary Ronberg, *NHL: The World of Professional Ice Hockey* (New York: Gallery Books, 1981), p. 193.

Chapter 6. Ready to Launch

1. Personal interview with Roger Neilson, April 1998.

2. *Philadelphia Flyers 1996–97 Yearbook*, p. 47.

3. Personal interview with Roger Neilson.

GLOSSARY

assist—The action of a player, usually a pass, that allows a teammate to score a goal.

backhand—Any shot or pass made with the stick turned around.

center—The job of the center is usually to set up the wingers for shots, and to take face-offs.

defenseman—The player whose main job is to stop the opposing team's forwards from getting good shots on goal.

forechecking—The act of checking an opponent while the opponent is still in the defensive zone.

goalie—The player whose main responsibility is to stay in front of the net and deflect or block the opposing team's shots.

line—Arrangement of three forwards or two defensemen who go out on the ice to play for shifts of roughly two minutes each.

period—A twenty-minute span. A standard hockey game has three periods.

point—A player is given a point whenever that person scores a goal or records an assist. Teams also earn points. A win is worth two points, and a tie is worth one point in the standings. The point totals are used to determine playoff seeding.

power play—A situation in which one team temporarily has an extra player (or players) on the ice because of a penalty on the other team.

Stanley Cup—The trophy presented annually to the NHL's playoff championship team.

winger—One of the offensive positions or players on either side of the center.

FURTHER READING

Diamond, Dan. ed. *The Official NHL Philadelphia Flyers Quiz Book*. Plattsburgh, N.Y.: McClelland and Stewart Tundra Books, 1994.

Greenberg, Jay. *Full Spectrum: The Complete History of the Philadelphia Flyers Hockey Club*. Chicago: Triumph Books, 1996.

Hochman, Stan. *The Sports Book: Everything You Need to Be a Fan in Philadelphia*. Norristown, Pa.: PB Publications, Inc., 1995.

Hollander, Zander, ed. *Inside Sports Hockey*. Detroit: Visible Ink Press, 1997.

Kreiser, John. *Eric Lindros*. Broomall, Pa.: Chelsea House Publishers, 1997.

Rappoport, Ken. *Sports Great Eric Lindros*. Springfield, N.J.: Enslow Publishers, Inc., 1997.

Rennie, Ross. *The Philadelphia Flyers*. Mankato, Minn.: Creative Education, Inc., 1990.

Stewart, Mark. *Eric Lindros*. Danbury, Conn.: Children's Press, 1997.

INDEX

A
Angotti, Lou, 12
Atlanta Flames, 30

B
Barber, Bill, 8, 32
Boston Bruins, 12, 18, 30
Bowman, Scotty, 26
Brind'Amour, Rod, 6–8, 39
Buffalo Sabres, 26, 30
Bunyan, Paul, 21

C
Clarke, Bobby, 8, 13, 15, 17, 21, 31–33, 35
Conn Smythe Trophy, 17, 21
CoreStates Center, 8
Crozier, Roger, 31

D
Desjardins, Eric, 7, 17, 35, 36, 39
Detroit Red Wings, 6, 36
Driver, Bruce, 8
Dupont, Andre "Moose," 15, 30

E
Eastern Conference Finals, 5, 8
Edmonton Oilers, 21, 27, 29

F
Flin Flon, Manitoba, Canada, 13, 32
Florida Panthers, 7

G
Gratton, Chris, 37
Gretzky, Wayne, 8, 21, 27

H
Hall, Glenn, 18
Hart Trophy, 32
Hextall, Ron, 7, 15, 21, 26
Hockey Hall of Fame, 8, 12, 18, 32
Howe, Gordie, 37
Howe, Mark, 17

K
Keenan, Mike, 26, 27
Kelly, Bob, 15, 30, 31
Kerr, Tim, 15, 17

L
Leach, Reggie, 32
LeClair, John, 6, 15, 35–37, 39
Legion of Doom, 36
Lemieux, Mario, 37
Lindbergh, Pelle, 15, 18, 19, 21
Lindros, Eric, 5–6, 9, 15, 17, 37, 39

M
MacLeish, Rick, 32
Marsh, Brad, 27
Messier, Mark, 6, 37
Montreal Canadiens, 15, 24, 35, 36
Murphy, Larry, 36

N
Neilson, Roger, 36, 39
New Jersey Devils, 29
New York City, 11
New York Islanders, 26
New York Rangers, 5, 6, 8, 30

O
Olajuwon, Hakeem, 21
Orr, Bobby, 30

P
Parent, Bernie, 8, 12, 17, 18, 31, 32
Peeters, Pete, 15
Philadelphia Inquirer, 30
Philadelphia Quakers, 11
Prince of Wales Trophy, 9
Propp, Brian, 15

Q
Quebec City, 12
Quebec Nordiques, 37
Quinn, Pat, 24–26

R
Recchi, Mark, 35
Renberg, Mikael, 36, 37
Richter, Mike, 5, 8
Rochefort, Leon, 12

S
St. Louis Blues, 13, 15
Saleski, Don, 30
Schultz, Dave, 15, 23, 29
Shero, Fred, 23, 24, 29, 33
Snider, Ed, 11, 15
Soviet Union, 24
Spectrum, 12, 19
Stanley Cup, 8, 9, 12, 15, 23, 30, 33, 39
Stanley Cup Finals, 6, 15, 21, 24, 26, 30, 35
Sweden, 18, 36

T
Taylor, Bobby, 18
Therien, Chris, 7, 39

V
Van Impe, Ed, 17
Vermont, 36
Vezina Trophy, 17, 19, 21

WHERE TO WRITE

Philadelphia Flyers
CoreStates Center
One CoreStates Complex
Philadelphia, PA 19148

WEB SITES

http://www.nhl.com/teams/phi/index.htm
http://espn.go.com/nhl/clubhouses/phi.html

The Philadelphia Flyers Hockey Team

RENFROE MIDDLE SCHOOL
280 WEST COLLEGE AVE.
DECATUR, GEORGIA 30030